The Big Basketball Prize

by MARION RENICK

Illustrated by PAUL GALDONE

CHARLES SCRIBNER'S SONS · New York

At Timmy's house the boys were shooting basketballs. Becky watched them aim at the hoop on the garage. Big Red, the high school boy from next door, made a perfect shot every time. Greg made some good ones too. Timmy always missed. He couldn't even run after the ball without tripping over his feet.

"I give up," Timmy said. "Why can't I play better?"

"Maybe your feet are too big," said Becky.

"Maybe you need a shopping bag to catch the ball," Greg laughed.

"What you need is Perfect Muscular Control. Like this." Big Red flipped the ball through the hoop with one hand.

"Wow!" Timmy and Greg shouted.

"That's what you'll need in the Basketball Contest," Big Red said. "You boys are going into it, aren't you?"

"Not me," Timmy muttered. He could never get the ball through the hoop.

"You'll miss a lot of fun," said Big Red. "One of you might even win the big basketball prize. All you need is Perfect Muscular Control."

"What *is* that stuff?" Timmy asked.

Big Red bounced the ball, spun around and sent it right square through the hoop. "That's what it is. See?"

Timmy tried it. He missed the hoop and scared a bird
out of its bath. "See *that?* I give up."

"Aw, don't!" Greg said. "We can have fun if we go
in the Contest together. Keep on trying."

Timmy ran to get the ball. He stumbled and fell. He
skinned both knees. So he went home.

"Tsk, tsk," Mother said as she took care of his cuts. "You're always hurting yourself. Poor Timmy."

"I'm not poor Timmy at all. I'm just awkward. That's what Greg and Becky say." Suddenly he felt tears in his eyes. "M-m-maybe I'm t-t-too awk-awkward to be a b-b-basketball player."

"Nonsense!" Mother patted him. "You'll outgrow being awkward."

"How soon?" he asked.

"Next year, perhaps." She smiled. "Don't worry about it."

But he did worry. Next year was too late for him. The Basketball Contest was this spring. He needed help *now*.

So he went to see his Grandmother Hinkle. Gran helped him lots of times. She never told anyone about it.

Gran was in her kitchen stirring something in a yellow bowl. "Hi, Timmy," she said. "What's the trouble now?"

"Oh, Gran," he sighed. "I'm so awkward."

Gran laughed. "You'll outgrow it, dear."

"In time for the Basketball Contest?" he asked.

"Not quite that soon," she said.

"Then I may as well stay awkward." Timmy threw himself into a chair without looking first. Gran's cat leaped out just in time. *Mmm-rrr-ow!*

Grandmother Hinkle didn't look up. "A boy who wants to play basketball needs control," she said to the yellow bowl.

Timmy remembered Big Red's advice. "Perfect Muscular Control," he said. "The lucky boys have it. I never will."

"A fellow can get it if he wants it bad enough," Gran told him. "*You* could do it yourself."

"Really? In time for the Contest?"

"You can try." Gran set down the bowl and wiped her hands. "I'll give you a magic charm to help you. But first you must promise to use it as I say."

"I will, Gran! I promise!"

Gran went to the broom closet but stopped with her hand on the doorknob. "Remember, this charm will lose its <u>magic if</u> you break your word to me."

"I'll do everything you tell me to do with it. I promise," Timmy said again.

Gran opened the door. "Here you are." She brought out a rope. A plain ordinary rope. Sometimes she hung her washing on it.

Timmy stared at it. "Where's the magic in *that?*"

"The magic is in you," said Gran. "This rope is the charm to bring it out. First, we'll cut off a piece just long enough....There! Take this for your jumping rope. And jump it for a while every day."

"But, Gran—" Timmy stood with the rope in his hands. "I don't think this will help me at all."

"Ask your dad. He'll tell you many a fine athlete trains by skipping rope. Every single day," said Gran.

Timmy wrapped one end of it around each hand. He swung it over his head. He lassoed Gran—yellow bowl, big spoon and all.

"Don't go at it so hard." She laughed. "Sing as you swing. Here, I'll beat time for you." She began to tap on the bowl with her spoon, singing an old song:

Go tell Aunt Abbie, go tell Aunt Abbie,
Go tell Aunt Abbie, the old gray goose is dead.

Timmy found himself jumping in time with the tune. He tripped and stumbled but went on to the end.

"Try it again," Gran said. She sang new words this time.

Go tell Tim Hinkle, go tell Tim Hinkle,
Go tell Tim Hinkle, he must help himself.

"Did you see me, Gran?" Timmy shouted. "I hardly tripped once!"

"Timmy, you are less awkward already." Gran beamed. "Keeping time helps, doesn't it?"

He began to jump again. He and Gran both sang.

Go tell Tim Hinkle...

Timmy kept on jumping till the dishes danced on the shelves and the cups almost hopped off their little hooks. Then Gran sent him outside to skip.

He set out singing and jumping and watching his feet.
Suddenly he stopped cold. He heard girls giggling.

There were Becky and her friends, *jumping rope!*
"Doesn't he look funny!" The girls laughed. Then away
they skipped, with a ha, ha, ha.

Only Becky didn't laugh. She stopped to say, "I'll
jump doubles with you, Timmy, if you want me to."

"Who said I want to jump at all?" He threw down
the rope and stomped off.

"Hi, Timmy!" somebody called. A car stopped. Big Red swung open the door. "Want a ride home?"

Then he saw the rope. "If that's yours, bring it along," he told Timmy. "I trained for basketball by jumping rope. You should try it too."

"That's what I'm doing," said Timmy.

"You'll have to learn to shoot baskets too, of course. I'll show you how." Big Red stopped in front of Timmy's house. "It just so happens that I have a ball here—" He opened the door to the back seat and basketballs spilled out like beans when the bag breaks.

"Wow!" Timmy shouted. "There're hundreds of 'em!"

"Only twenty-four." Big Red laughed as he helped Timmy put them back. "They're from school. It's my job to clean them up and pick out the good ones for the Basketball Contest."

"Are you going in the Contest, Red?"

"No, I'm too old. Besides, I won it once." He gave Timmy a little poke with his elbow. "You'll have to go into it this year and take my place. How about that?"

"I'll try!" Timmy was so excited he couldn't say anything more. "I'll try!"

Big Red headed for the hoop over the garage door. "The first thing to learn, Timmy, is *to watch what you're shooting at*. Now, it's the rim of the basket up there. Hold the ball in front of your neck and look up at the hoop. Only your fingers and thumbs touch the ball. This way. Keep your elbows cocked, your back straight. Face the hoop squarely and bend your knees a little. Keep thinking all the time: *I'm going to put this ball up there easy.* Then, whammie! Fingers, elbows, knees snap straight all together. And you *push* that ball right up there. See?"

Up it went, and dropped down through the hoop.

Timmy caught it on the second bounce.

"Let me try it!"

Big Red laid a stick in the drive. "For a foul line," he said. "Stand with your toes back of it and shoot for the hoop. That's how they shoot free throws in games. And in the Contest."

Timmy got set. He gave the ball a push, but it flew past the hoop and sent a squirrel scampering. He tried again. This time the ball swished through the basket.

He practiced for a long time. He jumped rope too. *Go tell Tim Hinkle...he must help himself.*

Day after day he worked hard. Then one day he missed the hoop ten times in a row. He picked up the ball and went to tell Greg, "I give up. I'm not going in the Contest."

"You said you would," Greg reminded him. "Think of the fun we'll have."

"What fun will it be for me? I'll lose out in Round 1." Timmy aimed the ball at the hoop. "I'll miss my very first shot. Like this." He shot, and—

"Good one!" He heard Becky call. She was walking by with her dog. She stopped to lead a cheer. "Ya-a-ay, Timmy!"

"I'll bet you can make another good one," Greg said.

"I'll bet I can't," said Timmy. He stood very still and aimed carefully. His shot was perfect.

"You're both beginning to look like basketball players," Becky said. "But, Timmy, why don't you shoot the way Greg does?"

"I shoot fouls like my dad," said Greg. He stooped, holding the ball almost to his knees. He swung it up and sent it sailing through the hoop. "That's the way he showed me."

"Big Red says a player is allowed to shoot free throws any way he can make 'em," Timmy said. The boys told Becky, "A player can win the game sometimes just by making his foul shot good." This thought started them shooting at the basket again.

They kept Becky busy running after the ball. Her dog ran after it too. "I'm surprised you don't trip over him," she said to Timmy. "You aren't so awkward as you used to be. How come?"

Timmy didn't say. It was his secret and he wouldn't tell.

From then on he and Greg were always together, working at basketball. They began to think the Contest was *theirs*.

They discovered they were wrong. One day they took the long way home from school. At almost every house they saw boys throwing balls at a hoop on the garage. Even Big Red was practicing. "I'm glad *he* won't be in the Contest!" Greg said.

They counted Red's throws till he missed.

"Sixteen!" Timmy shouted. "That is sharp shooting!"

"Perfect Muscular Control!" Greg yelled.

Big Red laughed. "And don't you forget it. That's what will win the Contest."

"Suppose all the boys have it?" Timmy asked. "Suppose there are eighty or ninety sharp shots trying to win?"

"Don't think about them," Red said. "Keep your eyes on the hoop and push the ball up there. Like this. See?"

At last the day of the Contest arrived.

Timmy and Greg went to the high school. Becky tagged along. They saw a huge sign on the building.

10th Annual
BASKETBALL FOULSHOOTING
CONTEST!

As they walked into the gym, Big Red called, "Hi, Timmy! Hi, Greg!" He took the boys over to some men at a long table.

One man wrote down each boy's name and age. "Draw a number from the box and pin it on your back," he said.

Greg reached in. His piece of paper had "1" on it. Timmy drew "13."

"Uh-oh! That's unlucky!" A shout went up from the boys around him. "Thirteen is an unlucky number!"

They showed him all kinds of things *they* had to bring them luck: bow ties, rabbits' feet, patched shorts and bright shirts. A boy named Sligo wore a hat with a long skinny blue plume, a pair of dice and a little horseshoe on it. Another boy had on one red sock and one blue one for luck.

"What have you got to bring *you* luck?" he asked Timmy.

"He's got nothing but that 13!" Sligo laughed. "He'll be out of the Contest this fast." He gave Timmy a shove. He shoved Greg too. The tall blue plume in his hat danced. Greg muttered to Timmy, "That Sligo thinks he's won the prize already."

"Here we go, boys!" The man at the table pointed across the wide floor. "Line up by number in front of that basket."

Timmy had never shot at this kind of basket. This was no hoop on a garage. It had a glass backboard, and *nothing* underneath. "I don't think I can shoot without a wall in front of me," he said to Greg.

"Me either," Greg said.

Big Red gave the rules. "Each boy gets one shot at the basket. If you make it, you stay in the Contest for the next round. As soon as you miss, you're out. Sudden death."

He smiled. "So don't hurry. Take time for your shot. Keep your toes back of the foul line. Don't bother a boy when he is shooting. Okay? Let's go! Step to the foul line, Number 1."

"Who, me?" Greg squeaked. "You mean I have to start this?"

"I'm glad I'm 13, unlucky or not," Timmy said to himself.

"Here's the ball!" One of the men threw it to Greg.

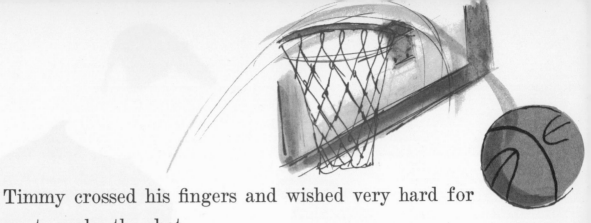

Timmy crossed his fingers and wished very hard for Greg to make the shot.

Greg missed.

"Too bad." The man patted Greg's shoulder and sent him to the side lines. "Better luck next year."

Timmy shivered.

The second boy made his shot. Numbers 3 and 4 missed. Timmy felt a bump from the boy behind him. He looked around. It was Sligo, shoving again.

How can a fellow shoot with that going on, Timmy wondered. He remembered what Big Red had said: *Don't think about the others.*

So Timmy didn't even watch to see if Number 12's foul was good. When "13" was called, he walked to the line keeping his eyes on the basket. With the ball in his hands, he took time to think how he would lay it up there. He cocked his elbows and bent his knees a little. He gave the ball a quick push. Into the basket it went!

Whee-yoo! He took a good long breath. He was still in the Contest!

His second shot was good too. After five more rounds only a few boys were left. Timmy was still in. And Sligo, behind him.

Timmy felt great. He had made seven baskets! He got set for his next shot, humming: *Go tell Tim Hinkle, he can make one more.*

Just as he was shooting, something sailed past his ear and spoiled his aim. The ball missed the basket.

"Sudden death" for Timmy.

He walked away with his head down. There on the floor he saw Sligo's hat. *That's what spoiled my shot,* he thought.

"Timmy!" he heard Big Red call. "Wait a minute!"

Timmy turned back. The man in charge was talking to Sligo. "I wasn't throwing my hat at *him,*" Sligo said. "I was throwing it to the fellows on the side lines to keep for me. It kind of gets in my way when I shoot."

"Whatever you were doing, you spoiled 13's shot," the man said.

"He might have missed anyway." Sligo threw Timmy
a look.

"True," said the man. "But you broke a rule of sports-
manship. You should have stood still while he was shooting. You want the other boys to do that for *you,* don't
you?"

The man picked up Sligo's hat and nodded at Timmy.
"Take your shot over, 13."

This was a hard one to make. Timmy knew everybody was watching. He didn't look anywhere except at that basket up there. He pretended it was the one on the garage at home. He took aim, sent the ball spinning—then heard Becky shout, "Good one!" She and Greg cheered, "You're still *in,* Timmy! *Rah, rah, rah!*"

Sligo's turn came. He strutted to the foul line, cocky as ever....He missed. He grabbed his hat and slammed it on his head. He left the gym with the blue plume hanging down his back.

At the end of the next round, only Timmy and the boy with the lucky socks were left. Timmy was so tired he felt he couldn't push the ball up there another time. But he did.

The ball hung on the hoop—*Timmy froze*—then it dropped in.

The other boy missed. Timmy was the winner!

Newsmen came with cameras. Big Red, all smiles, gave him the great golden Winner's Cup. He winked at Timmy when the newsmen asked, "How did you win your very first Contest?"

Timmy winked back. Then he answered loud and clear, "Perfect Muscular Control."

JF
REN

Renick
  The big basketball prize